Animales del zoológico / Zoo Animals

LOS RENOS
REINDEER
AT THE ZOO

Seth Lynch
Traducido por / Translated by Esther Ortiz

Gareth Stevens
PUBLISHING

Please visit our website, www.garethstevens.com. For a free color catalog of all our high-quality books, call toll free 1-800-542-2595 or fax 1-877-542-2596.

Library of Congress Cataloging-in-Publication Data

Names: Lynch, Seth, author.
Title: Los renos / Reindeer at the zoo / Seth Lynch.
Description: New York : Gareth Stevens Publishing, [2020] | Series: Animales del zoológico / Zoo animals | Includes index.
Identifiers: LCCN 2018039583| ISBN 9781538243640 (library bound)
Subjects: LCSH: Reindeer–Juvenile literature. | Zoo animals–Juvenile literature.
Classification: LCC QL737.U55 L96 2020 | DDC 599.65/8–dc23
LC record available at https://lccn.loc.gov/2018039583

First Edition

Published in 2020 by
Gareth Stevens Publishing
111 East 14th Street, Suite 349
New York, NY 10003

Translator: Esther Ortiz
Editor, English: Therese Shea
Designer: Katelyn E. Reynolds

Photo credits: Cover, p. 1 Nadezda Nikitina/Shutterstock.com; p. 5 Theodor Negru/Shutterstock.com; p. 7 Iordache Elena G/Shutterstock.com; pp. 9, 24 (moss) Jeremy-Stenuit/Shutterstock.com; p. 11 Annettt/Shutterstock.com; p. 13 Sergey Gordienko/Shutterstock.com; pp. 15, 24 (hoof) Tagwaran/Shutterstock.com; p. 17 Bogorodskiy/Shutterstock.com; pp. 19, 24 (antler) vadimmva/Shutterstock.com; p. 21 Olenyok/Shutterstock.com; p. 23 Shestock/Blend Images/Getty Images.

Printed in the United States of America

CPSIA compliance information: Batch #CS19GS: For further information contact Gareth Stevens, New York, New York at 1-800-542-2595.

Contenido

Aprendamos sobre los renos 4
Renos hambrientos 8
El cuerpo de los renos 12
Los cuernos 18
Me gustan los renos 22
Palabras que debes aprender 24
Índice 24

Contents

Learning About Reindeer 4
Hungry Reindeer 8
Reindeer Bodies 12
Antlers 18
I Like Reindeer! 22
Words to Know 24
Index 24

Veo renos
en el zoológico.
¡Aprendo mucho!

I see reindeer
at the zoo.
I learn a lot!

Los renos son
un tipo de venado.

....

Reindeer are
a kind of deer.

Comen plantas.
Comen pasto y musgo.

They eat plants.
They eat grass and moss.

¡Excavan para buscar comida!

They dig for food!

Tienen pelaje.
Los mantiene abrigados.

....

They have fur.
It keeps them warm.

Tienen pezuñas.
Pueden caminar
sobre el hielo.

They have hooves.
They can walk
on ice.

!Pueden nadar!

They can swim!

Les crecen cuernos.
¡Los cuernos son huesos!

They grow antlers.
Antlers are bone!

Los cuernos se caen
cada año.
¡Los animales se
los comen!

....

Antlers fall off
each year.
Animals eat them!

Me gustan los renos
del zoológico.

....

I like the reindeer
at the zoo!

Palabras que debes aprender
Words to Know

(el) cuerno
antler

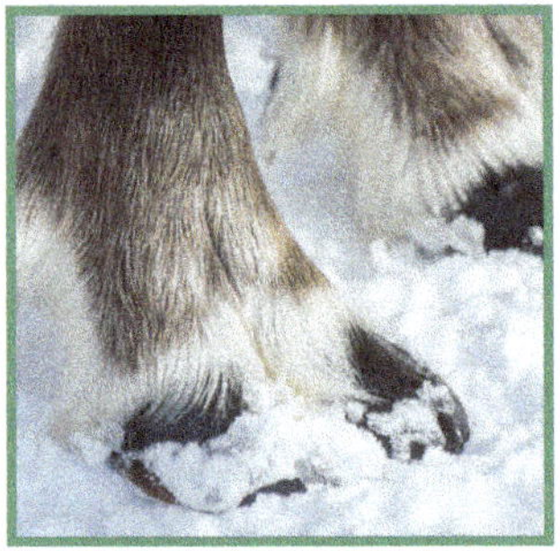

(la) pezuña
hoof

(el) musgo
moss

Índice/Index

cuerno / antler 18, 20

pelaje / fur 12

pezuñas / hooves 14

plantas / plants 8